Impatient Pamela®

Wants a BIGGER Family

Impatient Pamela

Wants a BIGGER Family

Mary Koski

ILLUSTRATED BY Dan Brown

Trellis Publishing, Inc.

P.O. Box 16141
Duluth, MN 55816
800-513-0115

Impatient Pamela® Wants a BIGGER Family

Publisher's Cataloging-in-Publication

Koski, Mary (Mary B.)
    Impatient Pamela Wants A Bigger Family/
    by Mary Koski ; illustrated by Dan Brown.
    p. cm.
    SUMMARY: Pamela visits her friend Sam's house and learns the delights of a large family, but finally realizes being an only child is special too.

    LCCN: 2002091088
    ISBN: 1-930650-04-3
    1. Only child - fiction.
    2. Adoption - fiction.
    3. Family size - fiction.

PZ7.K85Imb 2002   [E]
    I. Brown, Dan (Daniel Seaton) II. Title.

10 9 8 7 6 5 4 3 2 1
Printed in China

Cover designed by George Foster, Interior designed by Dan Brown

Dedicated to my mother and father, who managed their ever-so-large family of seven children

M. Koski

Dedicated to my friends and family who have inspired and supported me throughout the years

D. Brown

Pamela really liked her friend Sam. He played a good game of checkers, and he understood the beauty of her stamp collection. But being at his house, now that was an adventure.

You see, Sam had seven brothers:
Manuel, Ken, Kim, Billy, Bobby, Ben and Florian.

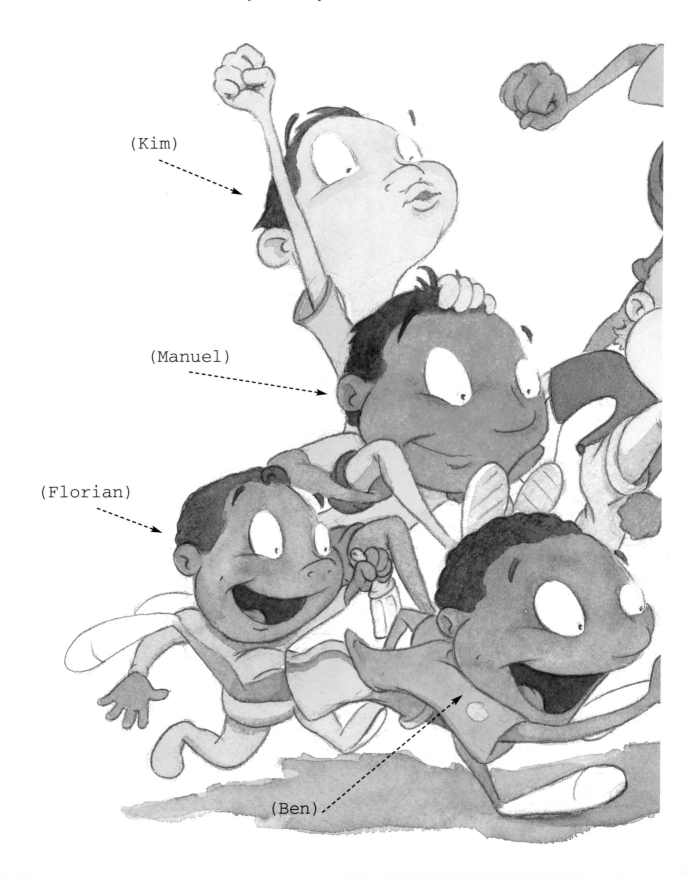

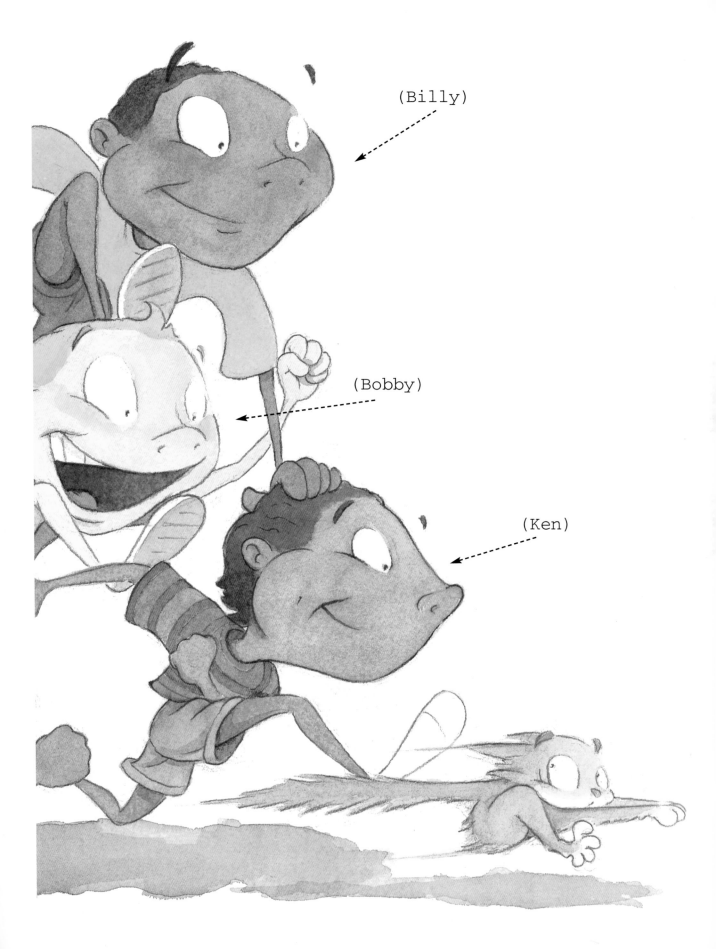

(Billy)

(Bobby)

(Ken)

"Momma," Pamela asked her mom one day, "how does Sam cope with having seven brothers?"
"I don't know, Pamela. Why do you ask?"

"Because he invited me over for lunch tomorrow. I don't know if we'll all fit in the kitchen. I've never eaten there before. It might be a mess."
"Pamela, you could end up having a great time. I think you should go and find out. Being part of a large family can be very exciting."

So Pamela went to lunch. First, she took off her shoes in the entryway. Shoes were piled high.

"Hey Sam," she asked, "why do you have seven brothers?"

"I don't know," Sam shrugged.

"And why are these shoes so messy?" Pamela asked.

"Because, we're just going to put them on again after lunch. Let's go eat."

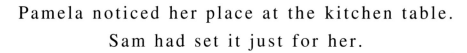

Pamela noticed her place at the kitchen table.
Sam had set it just for her.

Pamela

Everyone started passing the food
around the table.

"Pass the pancakes please," Pamela said.
Nothing happened. She tried saying it a little
louder. "Pass the pancakes, please."
"PANCAKES PLEASE," Sam shouted. Sam's
father laughed at baby Florian who was
learning his first words.
And Sam's mother argued with
Manuel, who wanted to drink pop
for lunch. Sam's mother just kept
saying "no, no, no." Bobby
passed the pancakes.

Don't you get in trouble for shouting at the table?"
Pamela asked quietly.

"If you don't speak up, you won't get anything around
here. Mom and Dad say to speak up when you need
something," Sam said.

Pamela liked the idea of speaking up.

Pamela was impatient to know why
Sam had seven brothers. So she
decided to speak up.
Right now.

How come
Sam has seven
brothers?!

Pamela
loved speaking
up. Manuel, Ken,
Kim, Billy,
Bobbie, Ben, and
Florian all smiled
at Pamela. Sam
looked a little
startled.

"Well Pamela," Sam's mother said,   "Manuel, Ken, Kim, Bobby, Ben and Florian were adopted, and Billy and Sam were born to us. Adopted means we chose some children to come and be a part of our family. We became their parents, and we take care of them. We always wanted a large family."

Pamela was surprised. She'd never heard about being adopted before.

"Is there anything hard about having seven brothers?" Pamela asked Sam later.
"Well, somebody's always borrowing your clean shirts and socks . . ."

". . . and you have to wait in line to use the bathroom in the morning . . ."

". . . and if everyone is playing in the house because it's raining or cold outside, it gets kind of loud. And if mom calls us, she can get all mixed up in her names and go through the whole list . . .

. . . before she gets to the right person."

"And you never
have a room all to
yourself. Forget
that! We have the
big boys in one
room . . .

. . . and the small
boys in another."

"So what's good about having seven brothers?"
Pamela asked, thinking about how many players it
took for a game of softball.

"Sometimes, when one of us has been bad or gets in trouble, we all understand how he feels. Or if one of us does well, we celebrate together. Last week, Ken played a drum solo at the school band concert, and our parents clapped like crazy at the end. Then we all got to go out for treats."

"And there's always someone to play with, or talk to, or just be with. I like that the most." Pamela knew what he meant, because she often felt lonesome having only Meow-Man to play with.

Pamela decided that she wanted a bigger family. That night, she begged her mother, "Can't we have a bigger family? **Pleeeaasse?** I want some brothers, and maybe some sisters. I get lonesome, all by myself. How come we don't have more kids?"

"Families come in all sizes
Pamela, and we like this size.
Since our family is small we get
to spend more time with you,
and we love that. We get to help
you with your homework . . .

. . . and teach you how to grill fajitas . . ."

" . . . and come to most of your soccer games. If we had lots of children, we might not be able to spend that much time with each child."

"But just imagine, Momma. If we had more kids, we could
all do our homework together, and we could all cook
together, and we could all play soccer together. That
could be a lot of fun. I'd always have somebody to play
with. Let's have a bigger family.
We could adopt some kids. That's
what Sam's brothers mostly
are. Adopted. Am I adopted?"

"No, you're not adopted,
and we won't be adopting other
kids either. This is the family we have, Pamela. This is
the size it will stay. When you're lonesome, you can go
play with your friends, and you can always talk to us."

"No more kids?" Pamela asked sadly.

"No more kids."

Pamela felt a little disappointed. She fell asleep listening to the clock downstairs, and the purring of Meow-Man at her feet.

The next morning, Pamela woke up and went straight into the bathroom. She didn't have to wait in line.

She opened her dresser drawers, and all her clothes were there. No one had borrowed them. She dressed in her favorite pants and shirt. She listened to the music her dad was playing on the radio, and Pamela's mother told her all about the stories in the newspaper.

Pamela sat down at the breakfast table, and her
dad had all the dishes lined up and in place.
Everyone had their own spot.
Her mom fried the eggs.

Her parents argued about who was going to take Meow-Man in for his shots, but nobody shouted. At least, not too loudly. Pamela smiled.

This is special, too. This is my family. Kind of quiet, and maybe boring, but special.

"Pass the juice, please,"
Pamela said softly. Her mom
handed her the juice, and
they all talked about their
day.